Pip the Penguin

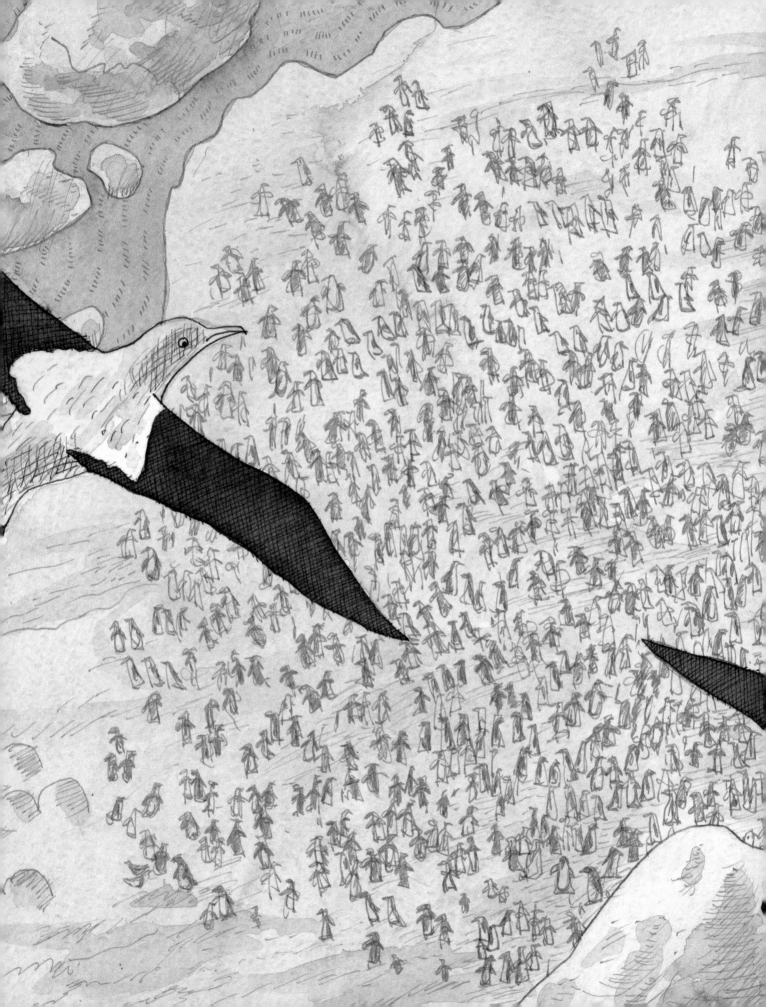

Pip

the

Penguin

Joy Cowley ★ Gavin Bishop

SCHOLASTIC INC.
New York Toronto London Auckland Sydney
Mexico City New Delhi Hong Kong Buenos Aires

In a fine penguin nest, a fine penguin egg
cracked open to show a beak and a leg.
A chick fell out of the egg with a flip.
"Pip!" he squeaked. "Pip, pip, pip!"

Ma and Pa Penguin shouted, "Oh joy!
Pip is the name of our baby boy.
Now we must warn our darling child
of the dangers in our Antarctic wild."

4

"**Danger one** is a skua with a nasty beak.
It looks for chicks that are small and weak.

Danger two is as bad. It's a hungry seal
that likes nothing more than a penguin meal."

"**Danger three**, in the sea, is a killer whale.
The penguin it meets will not tell the tale."

8

"**Danger four** is a snowstorm — and that's not nice.
It will freeze your feathers and turn you to ice."

"So, little Pip, don't be tempted to roam.
The safest place is home, sweet home.
Be happy here and forget the rest.
Nest is best. Yes, nest is best."

Little Pip stayed in the nest all alone,
while Ma and Pa caught fish on their own.
But Pip got bored by himself all day,
with nowhere to go and nowhere to play.

So, one grey morning, he waddled down
the rocky slope to Penguin Town.
All around him were scattered nests of chicks,
squawking penguins and squeaking chicks.

13

Then came a wild scream out of the sky!
Pip jumped in a nest as a skua swooped by.
But a penguin pushed him out of the nest.
"Don't come here! You're not my guest!"

Pip waddled off and sat on a rock.
A moment later, he got a big shock.
The rock was warm, with a soft furry feel . . .

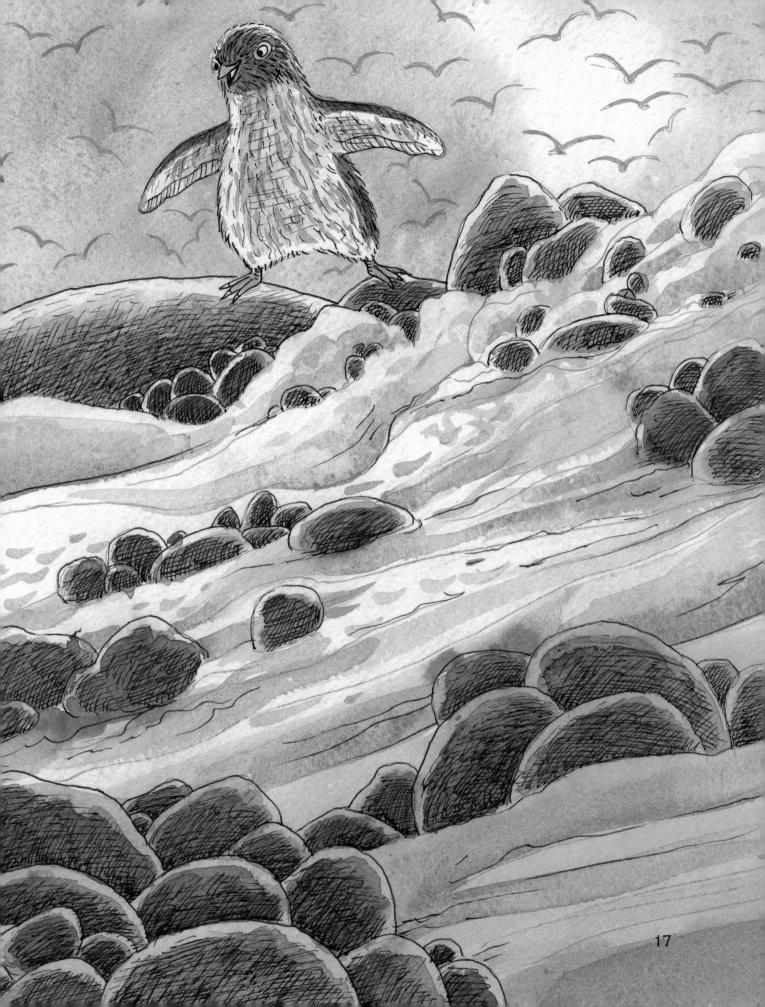

Pip was on top of a sleeping seal!

The seal gave a roar and, quick as a flea,
Pip took a tumble right into the sea.
He swam very fast, the seal at his tail . . .

right into the path of a killer whale.

Poor Pip just knew he was gone for good.
If the seal didn't get him, the killer whale would.
Oh, why had he left his fine little nest?
Didn't he know that nest was best?

A splashing and sploshing went over his head.
The whale was chasing the seal instead!
Pip swam ashore, still safe and sound,
and climbed out onto the stony ground.

22

But where was he now?
Which way should he go?
All he could see was whirling snow.
He'd escaped from a skua,
a seal and a whale . . .

24

now he was caught in an Antarctic gale.

Where was his nest? Was it near or far?
How would he find his Ma and Pa?
They had been right. It was wrong to roam
away from the safety of home, sweet home.

Then inside Pip's head,
like a warm little light,
came a voice that told him,
"This way is right.
Go straight ahead. Don't stop to rest.
This is the way back to your nest."

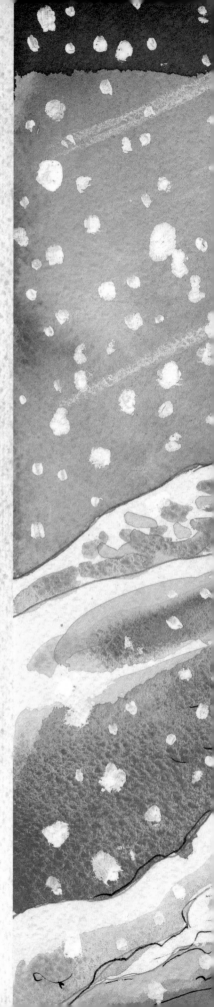

So Pip waddled on through ice and snow,
his instinct pointing the way to go,

and sure enough,
in the snow ahead,
he saw Ma and Pa
and his own dear bed.

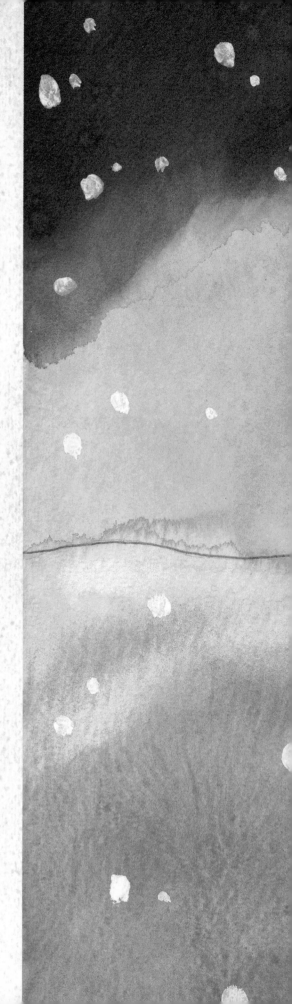

Oh, the squawking and oh, the joy
that met the return of the penguin boy!
His parents scolded with squeaks and hisses
and gave him lots of beaky kisses.

29

"I know," said Pip, "I've been a pest.
And you were right about our nest.
North or south, east or west,
nest is best. Yes . . .

nest is best!"

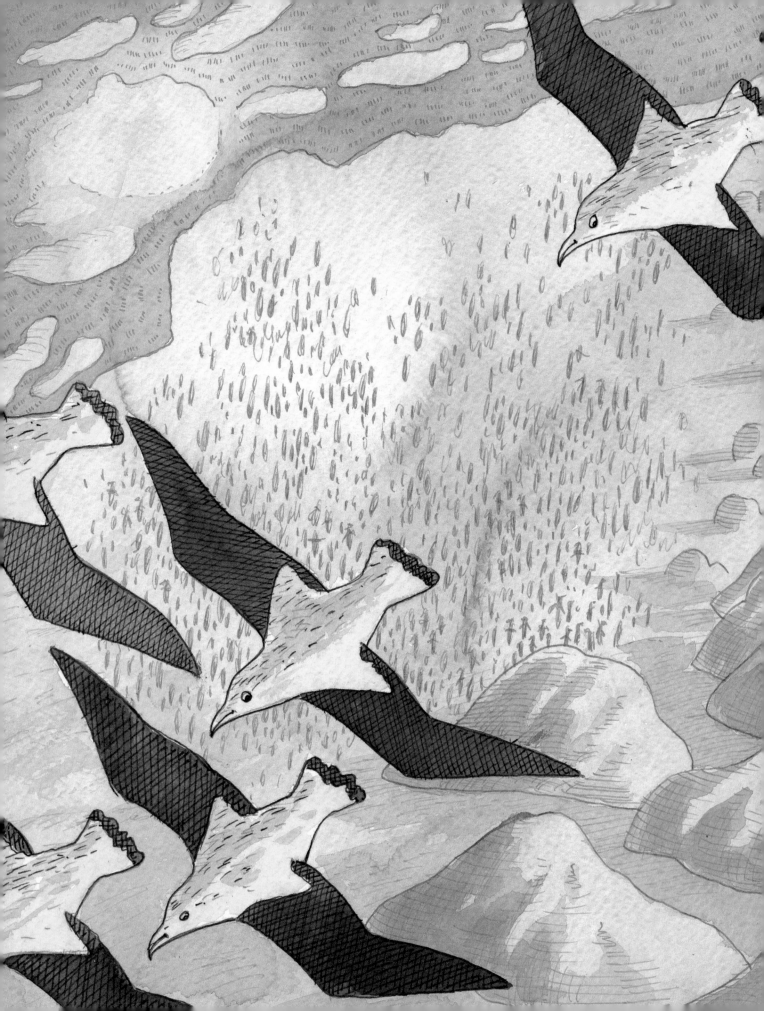

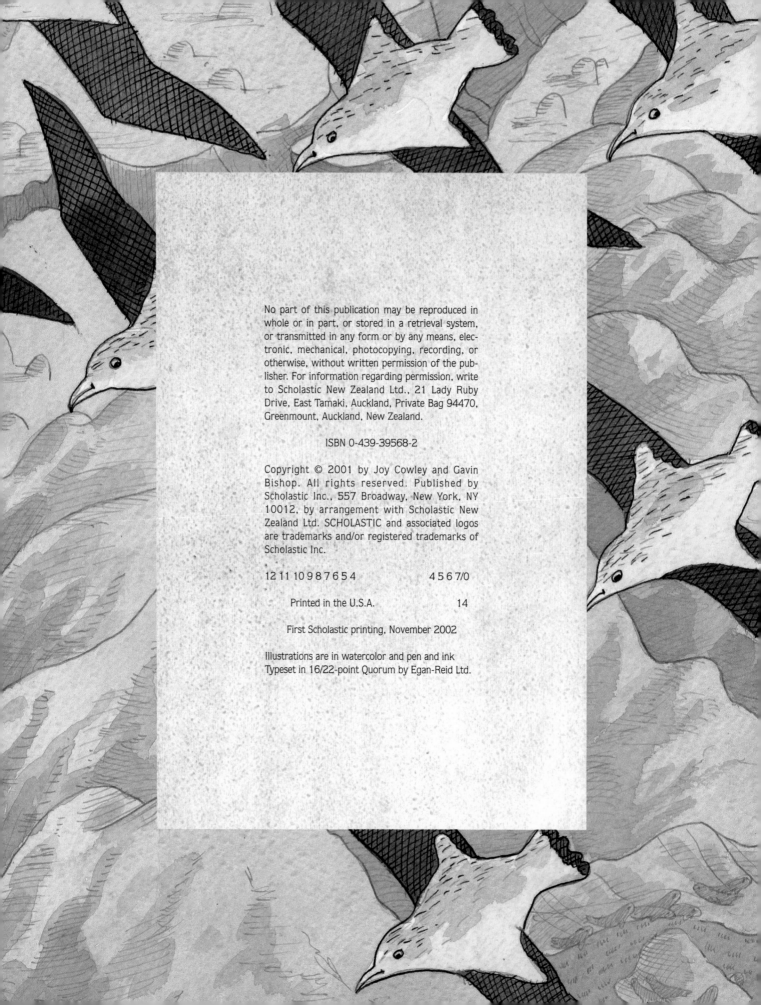

ISBN 0-439-39568-2

12 11 10 9 8 7 6 5 4   4 5 6 7/0

Printed in the U.S.A.   14

First Scholastic printing, November 2002

Illustrations are in watercolor and pen and ink
Typeset in 16/22-point Quorum by Egan-Reid Ltd.